W9-BUO-888

A Porc in New York

Catherine Stock

NEW YORK

1. Blooming Dells
2. Boat trip
3. Central Park
4. Mooma
5. Empire State Building
6. ~~Italian~~
   ~~Indian~~
   <u>Chinese</u> restaurant
7. Kool Kat Klub

Holiday House / New York

Bienvenue Jaden

Library of Congress Cataloging-in-Publication Data

Stock, Catherine.
A porc in New York / by Catherine Stock. — 1st ed.
p. cm.
Summary: Monsieur Monmouton and his dog Cabot fly from France to New York City
in pursuit of his farm animals, who are taking a vacation to see such sights as Blooming Dells and MOOMA.

ISBN-13: 978-0-8234-1994-4 (hardcover)
ISBN-10: 0-8234-1994-0 (hardcover)

[1. Domestic animals—Fiction. 2. Vacations—Fiction. 3. New York (N.Y.)—Fiction.] I. Title.

PZ7.S8635Por 2007

[E]—dc22
2006002015

Something was definitely up in the barn, in spite of Monsieur Monmouton's very firm "*Non!*" when the airline tickets the animals had ordered arrived in the post. The spree in Paris had been quite enough of an outing for this little farm.

Nevertheless, on clear windless nights, Monsieur Monmouton distinctly heard strange chanting drifting over from the barn:

"Two 'ot dogs with mustard pleeeze?"

"Taxi, Toity-toid and Toid pleeze?"

And sometimes even raucous singing:

"Noo Yawk, NOO YAWK!"

Monsieur Monmouton sent Cabot, his faithful shepherd dog, over to investigate. But the animals were always fast asleep in their stalls.

One fine morning, Monsieur Monmouton opened his barn to find it empty.
A scrawled note was pinned to a beam:

"*Ma foi!*" exclaimed
Monsieur Monmouton.
"What are the animals
up to now?"
Cabot, snuffling around
the straw, suddenly unearthed
a mysterious list:

Cabot brought the evidence to Monsieur Monmouton,
who ran back to his house and checked his rubbish bin.
The airplane tickets to New York were gone!
"Vite! Vite!" he shouted to Cabot, jumping into his old
truck. "We have to find the animals before the plane leaves!"

At the airport, a strange group of tourists excitedly trotted and waddled onto a plane.

A few minutes later, Monsieur Monmouton's truck screeched to a halt in front of the airport.

"Stop that plane!" he shouted.

"*Non, non, monsieur,* you'll have to catch the next plane," insisted the airline agent to the spluttering farmer.

Monsieur Monmouton and Cabot hurried to book the tickets.

At least they had the list to help them find the animals in New York.

As soon as the animals landed, the sheep insisted
on starting their tour at Blooming Dells.

    They hid quickly when Monsieur Monmouton and
Cabot hurried into the department store.

Cabot and Monsieur Monmouton arrived at the dock just as the animals, led by the geese, set off on a boat tour around Manhattan.

The goats treated everyone to a ride on the carousel in Central Park.

Woah! Monsieur Monmouton got so dizzy that the animals escaped again.

The cows led everyone around the new MOOMA museum.
The animals were nowhere to be seen as Monsieur Monmouton
puffed up the steps.

The pigeons fluttered impatiently. It was time for the Empire State Building. The sheep were disappointed not to find King Kong at the top.

Monsieur Monmouton's elevator rose quickly to the Observation Deck on the eighty-sixth floor as another noisy elevator with *moos*, clucks, *baas*, and grunts descended to the street.

Then the ravenous pigs hustled everyone down to Chinatown, where they wrestled with chopsticks.

Poor Monsieur Monmouton. He had no idea which Chinese restaurant to search! Cabot checked the list.

Then he stuck his paw into his mouth, whistled down a taxi, and shoved Monsieur Monmouton unceremoniously into the backseat.

Cabot pointed out the last item on the list to the taxi driver:

Kool Kat Klub.

"What a clever dog you are." Monsieur Monmouton sighed. "We will wait at this little corner table and catch those naughty rascals when they arrive."

"May I get you something?" inquired a pretty waitress.

"Ah *bon*, zank you, mademoiselle," stammered Monsieur Monmouton. His heart skipped a beat. "Two botteels of ginger ale, *s'il vous plaît*."

"Oh! You have such a lovely accent," purred the waitress. "Are you from France?"

Monsieur Monmouton blushed deeply and nodded.

The Kool Kats started playing some mellow jazz.

Half an hour later, in trooped an excited flurry of hens, sheep, chickens, cows, pigeons, goats, and pigs.

"*Salut mes amis*, come and join us," called Monsieur Monmouton, waving his bottle of ginger ale.

The animals couldn't believe their eyes.

"A round of ginger ale for my friends, *chérie!*"

Cabot dropped his head on his paws and sighed.

At the end of the last set, Cabot rounded up all the loudly protesting animals, and his even more loudly protesting farmer, and herded them out the door, to the airport, and onto the plane.

Four days after they got home, a fragrant postcard arrived in the mail.

The animals craned over Monsieur Monmouton's shoulders.

"*Chéri,*" it read, "*I have just bought a ticket to France. . . .*"